Airships

I shut my eyes and focused on the life I sensed. "Fire," I said softly, knowing Kena's sensitive were hearing was adequate. Moments later the roar of the cannons deafened all of us and Serpent Queen lurched sideways, rocking as the cannons recoiled.

Wood cracked and the enemy wounded screamed over the ringing in my ears. I heard a muffled "fire" and then the illusion hiding the enemy ship dropped. Dana gasped at the appearance of another dragon ship. Our maneuvers put it almost on top of us, but that was to their disadvantage. Serpent Queen's cannons had ripped the side of their hull badly.

"Dive." I tried not to let the tension I felt at the appearance of another dragon ship show. We could outrun zeppelin class ships, but we had no chance against another dragon class, loaded as we were.

Dana threw levers and spun the wheel. My ship dove, exposing her precious sails to the other ship's cannons, but they were still disorganized and the clouds thickened around us as Pint called more cover. The concussion of more cannons cracked the air and one split our topmost sail.

"Three Hells, dive!"

By J.A. Campbell

Inkwolf Press
Doc Vampire-Hunting Dog
Camping Tails
Mistaken Identities
Sheep Interrupted
Dog of the Dead
Doc's Dream Girl
The Moths of Miller Place

Sky Yarns
Serpent Queen

An Echelon Electric Short Series
Into the West #1 - #6

Published by Decadent Publishing
The Clanless #1 Senior Year Bites
The Clanless #2 Summer Break Blues

Stories Appearing in Other Anthologies
Brown, Ghost-Hunting Dog
The Saloon of Doom

The World of the Dreamkeepers
Darkness Taken

Roses for the Devil

By Full Moon's Light

Sky Yarns #1
Serpent Queen

By

J.A. Campbell

Inkwolf Press

For Sandra,
Enjoy!

Sky Yarns #1
Serpent Queen

An Inkwolf Press Novella

First Inkwolf Press Publication November 2012
All Rights Reserved.
Copyright © 2012 by J.A. Campbell
Cover Art © 2012 K.D. Howe

Published By: Inkwolf Press

ISBN-10: 148109744X
ISBN-13: 978-1481097444

PO Box 251
Severance, CO 80546-0251
Inkwolfpress@gmail.com
Inkwolfpress.com

Story by J.A. Campbell. World and Characters by
J.A. Campbell and S.N. Holl.

For Bobby

Your friendship, kindness and generosity are amazing. And your pirate parties rock!

ACKNOWLEDGMENTS

I've said it many times, but as solitary as writing is, no story is written alone. I want to thank my beta readers, Jen Wylie and Sam Knight, both talented writers along with being great beta readers. Go read their stuff! I also want to thank my line editors, D.F. Paul and Kimberly Carmen for their efforts on my behalf. You all caught silly mistakes, small errors and one really big one (Thanks Sam). Any remaining mistakes are all mine.

I want to thank the K.D. Howe team, Katie Parsons and Darren Howe, for the amazing cover. Serpent Queen sails dramatically against a Colorado sunset. The spectacular cover fills me with joy.

Thank you dearest readers for giving me a reason to keep writing my stories.

This world came about from an instant message conversation I had with my good friend S.N. Holl. She said "We need to make Vampire Steampunk a thing."

I replied, "Okay." Neither of us intended on building a world right then, but four hours later an idea turned into a world complete with a great cast of characters, religions, conflicts, an apocalypse, magic systems, everything you could possibly want in a steampunk world. And yes, Airships. Building a world like that is a heady experience, especially since we were on the same wavelength to the point where we would send each other the same idea at the same time. This novella and characters are very much mine, but S.N. Holl helped create the world and Bai Xiang, mentioned briefly in this story, is her character.

CHAPTER ONE

My eyes bled to black and the anticipation in her caramel eyes changed to delicious fear. Her lightly painted lips—parted in pleasure—widened, and she gasped, trying to pull away. I tightened my hand buried in her hair and held her close. I smiled, showing my fangs.

She whimpered, eyes darting to the side looking for a weapon, or escape. She opened her mouth wider to scream, and I put my finger over her lips.

"Shh, no need for that," I whispered.

The woman, barely old enough for my tastes, whimpered again, seeming to realize she was trapped. "Don't hurt me." Fear made her voice breathy.

She was a whore and I suspected she was used to men hurting her, but I wasn't interested in her body, just her blood. Clients who killed girls in the pleasure houses in the Ebony Kingdoms were themselves killed, but I could make people forget and she knew it. I let her fear linger a moment longer, drinking it like a fine liquor, before I relented.

"I won't hurt you, sweetling. Just a little blood. You won't remember a thing." I ran my finger over her lips, and then caressed her cheek before brushing her dark hair away from her eyes. A sheen of fear induced sweat covered her dark skin.

She relaxed and her eyes glazed as I took over her mind. Her soft moan made me briefly consider breaking my rule. I never slept with whores, just drank their blood. I kissed her gently on the neck, just over the strong pulse. Unable to restrain myself, I bit her.

She gasped in momentary pain, and then the venom in my saliva hit her system and her back arched in pleasure. I might have overdone it. I could control, to some degree, what my victims felt, but the hot rush of fresh blood made my mind fuzzy and she'd remember she had a good time. I pressed her against me as I drank, reveling in the heat of her body against my cooler flesh. Her breasts were small and firm, and her body was still fit and hadn't yet given into the ravages of time and her profession. I fought my desire, finally releasing her and stepping away. She sank back onto the bed, eyes glassy and lips parted slightly in ecstasy. I leaned against the wall and tried to collect myself. The way her breasts heaved under the thin, see-through fabric of her shift made that difficult, and I reluctantly turned away.

After a few minutes I regained control and knelt next to her, whispering in her ear. "You had a good time, but nothing unusual happened."

She moaned in pleasure. "You can visit any time, sailor."

I grinned and kissed her on the neck where I'd bitten her. Then I licked away the last of the blood, her wounds already closed. She'd have a slight bruise for a few hours but with her dark complexion no one would notice. I planted one more kiss softly on her lips, and suggested she sleep. I left a few extra coins on her dresser and slipped out of the pleasure house and into the muggy night of the Ebony Kingdoms.

I could count on one hand the number of humans who knew for certain I was a vampire outside of the Rom and my crew, and most of them were blood suppliers. More suspected I wasn't human, but there was little I could do about that. In many parts of the world being a known vampire was a death sentence. The Rom, well, they just always knew. It was best to stay away from them unless you'd already proved your worth. I fingered the small circle on the inside of my left wrist. It had a tiny rune in the center that always reminded me of a bird's wing, and meant I was a friend of the Rom.

The problem with being the captain of a high profile airship was that people knew who I was. If word got out I was less than human, well, that wouldn't go over so well. Of course, the rest of my officers were at least as interesting as I was. One of the many reasons we rarely took on passengers.

Port cities didn't slept and people from all over the world hurried on business despite the late hour. I took a few more random turns to confuse any possible pursuit, more out of habit than any suspicion of danger, and then headed back to the docks. The airship docks dominated the middle of town where natural rock outcroppings made convenient berths. This part of the Ebony Kingdoms was rocky desert instead of sand, and their monopoly on aether gas made any area with easily accessed airship docks an instant trade city.

I reached the lifts and paid the fee to ride. The wait was short and I stepped onto the open-air passenger lift and turned to watch the city as we rose into the air.

Most of the buildings were low and made of a local mud that helped keep the heat out during the day and the warmth in at night. Lights glittered from all parts of the town, though the richer areas were the darkest this time of night. The working class lived in the valley, and the wealthy in the heights. Even in the Ebony Kingdoms, they'd felt the affects of the magical leaks that had devastated the Tribunal's lands. The higher up you were, the safer. They didn't wall off most of the cities in the Kingdoms like they did further north, but you could still see the influence of the apocalypse.

The apocalypse was the foundation for the Tribunal's first and strongest rule: thou shalt not combine magic and machine. Some high level technomancer had screwed up and opened rifts into some other world. What came through those rifts was pretty terrible. Even though it was several hundred years ago I had vivid memories of the war. Scars from some clawed beast traced down my back and across my stomach if I ever needed a reminder—and vampires don't normally scar. These days the wilds were still dangerous but humanity had recovered and adapted with walls and technology and in some lands, magic.

Many smaller zeppelin class airships rested in their docks and I looked for anyone familiar as I left the lifts and passed them on my way to the larger berths. Many were in the process of refilling their dirigible air sacks and loading cargo. A few, ready to take off, strained at their mooring lines while they waited for clearance. I didn't recognize any of the ships in port, but I didn't get to this part of the Kingdoms very often. We were here for a very specific cargo from a sympathetic supplier.

There was little I loved more than my Serpent Queen, except maybe the remarkable woman I'd named my ship for. She was a dragon class airship and didn't have a dirigible air sack. She stored her aether gas in the hull and in the special paint on the steerage wings. Her sleek sails assisted maneuverability and she was far faster and agile than the zeppelin class ships. She was also more easily defended, as we didn't have to worry about a dirigible deflating. If our tanks were punctured, the gas would stay in the hull longer and keep us from crashing to the ground—in theory. I'd seen it both work and fail in practice.

The dockworkers finished the last touches of paint on the wings and someone had even slapped a fresh coat of paint on the trim and bowsprit. A beautiful dragon formed her figurehead. It was distinctive, which wasn't ideal for a pirate, but owning a dragon ship was distinctive enough as it was so I deemed the risk negligible. Besides, survivors were rare when we attacked another ship.

Two other people admired Serpent Queen. They wore the characteristic plain gray robes of Tribunal Penitents. Attention from the Tribunal was never good. Especially since I was about to smuggle an entire dragon shipload of aether gas into their countryside.

Transporting aether gas was problematic enough without having to fight other ships. The lighter than air substance allowed airships to float. Cooling and heating it reduced and increased the ship's buoyancy. Naturally a ship full of the gas would be very light if it was transported in its final state, and mostly unmanageable.

5

Therefore, we transported it as a liquid in separate tanks from the reagent that would turn it to gas when mixed. Aether liquid was still light though and we had to load ballast in the form of other cargo, but the payout from this run would be well worth the trouble. Especially since it would benefit the rebels too. Normally a shipload of aether gas would be more than any rebel group could afford, but they'd found a sympathetic ear in the Ebony Kingdoms and received a reduced rate.

I paused, debating if I should walk past the Penitents or sneak onto my ship. Unfortunately, I debated too long. One of the Tribunal mages turned and saw me. Resigned, I walked forward, trying to act as casual as I could. Physically, they didn't scare me, but I didn't want to have to kill them. That might get noticed.

"Eve'nin," I drawled as I walked past. It took them a second to realize I wasn't going to stop.

"Sir." One of the Penitents took a step toward me. I ignored them.

"You there, we're looking for the captain of this ship."

"Why?"

"The crew said he was gone and wouldn't let us board to wait for him."

I noticed they hadn't answered my question so I didn't quite answer theirs. "We don't deal with the Tribunal. We don't go into their airspace."

"I'd prefer to speak directly with the captain." The mage who spoke had a florid face and looked like he was commonly stressed out, but ate very well. The other, obviously from the northern lands as well, was more composed. They both wore the heavy robes that were all a

Penitent could wear per their religion. The robes were appropriate for the northern climates and travel by air, but even the cooler evenings here were too warm. I could smell their sweat over the sharp odor of freshly applied aether paint and thought there was more than one reason my crew hadn't wanted them onboard. My first mate, especially, had a very sensitive nose.

"That would be me."

The florid Penitent's disbelief was clear. I understood. In my loose linen clothing I didn't look like the captain of a dragon ship, but I did look a lot more appropriately dressed for the climate than they were.

"Very well, *Captain*. We can pay handsomely."

No doubt they wanted to ride on my ship because it was the nicest one in port. The Tribunal was snobbish like that. Of course, it could also be a trap.

"Sorry, not interested. We rarely deal with passengers, and we don't go to Tribunal airspace. That's final." Not legally anyway. I walked past them.

"It's almost as if you have something to hide." The quiet one finally spoke.

I shrugged. "Nope, just don't like the politics, the tariffs, or pretty much anything at all about the region and we don't need your money."

We usually ran a plank from the ship to the dock, but the extra aether gas on board floated the ship higher than normal, and prevented its use. I hoped the Penitents didn't notice or know enough about airships to realize it was unusual for my ship to be riding so high. The airman on deck recognized me when I hailed him and after accepting my all-clear hand sign, threw down the boarding ladder. It was rope and awkward to navigate if you weren't used to it, so I didn't think the Penitents would try to follow. I was halfway up when the florid one called out.

"Last chance to reconsider, Captain Adair. When we meet again, things won't go so easily for you."

Huh, they did know who I was. Probably a trap then. Chances were good they had an inkling of what we were up too as well. We'd need to be extra careful.

For once prudence won out, and I clamped my teeth shut to prevent an unwise reply. If my cargo could easily be replaced it wouldn't matter as much, but even I couldn't casually acquire another ship full of aether gas.

The airman pulled up the ladder as soon as I was on board. I nodded to him, and then braced myself as seventy pounds of Cathayan weather mage slammed into my leg.

Pint grinned up at me and I lifted her into the air and swung her around, carefully out of view of the Penitents below. Normally she would have giggled and yelled my name, but she knew when to be quiet. Pint had been with my crew for five years, the longest next to Robi, my quartermaster. As near as I could tell she was about ten. My lady dragon, Bai Xiang, sent her with me to save her from some undisclosed fate. She didn't call me father, but I was her only family. She was also extremely useful to have onboard. Pint's ability to control the weather rivaled all but some of the most experienced Cathayan Dragon Mages. A fact we kept well hidden.

I set her gently on the deck and she held my hand while we went back to the officers' cabins. Voices carried too easily at night and I didn't want to talk until we were inside.

"Kena and Dana got me a new dolly," she whispered while we walked.

I squeezed her hand. "Good. You'll have to show me."

Her smile got bigger. "She's a kitty like Kena."

I smiled. Kena, my first mate, was one of the most beautiful women I'd ever met, and I'd met a lot of women. Some of it had to do with her fierce personality, but her almost black skin, with lighter brown highlights when the sun hit it just right was stunning. Her high cheekbones and piercing black eyes made her exotic, especially when we were in the northern lands and, as Pint said, she was a were-jaguar. In human form she moved like a hunting cat, graceful and deadly, adding to her allure.

The Ebony Kingdoms were full of were-cats of all kinds, and the major religion in the Kingdoms was related to ancestor and cat worship. I was grateful to have Makena on board. She'd saved our asses more than once since she joined me a couple of years ago after I rescued her and my technomancer, Basil, from the Tribunal.

I led Pint to her room. As my second longest-term crewmember, and since she was essentially my ward, she rated a small room close to my own. Each officer had their own tiny cabin, and the crewmembers had berths below. Dana, my pilot, was asleep in her cabin and my sensitive vampire ears heard her gentle breathing as we walked past. Robi snored loudly, as usual. Kena paced in her room, waiting for my return and I tapped lightly on her door as I passed to let her know I was back. Basil wasn't in his room, but I wasn't worried. He rarely left the ship.

"Time for bed, Pint." I lifted her into her hammock.

"Will you tell me a story, Adair?"

"Not tonight, little one. Once we're in the air." I ruffled her short hair and kissed her forehead. She always waited up for me when I went out at night. I'd never been able to break her of that habit, and, finally, I'd stopped trying. "Maybe you can tell me a story too."

"And show you my new dolly." She yawned and snuggled into her blankets, asleep before I left the room.

"Makena," I greeted her as she stepped out of her cabin and followed me to mine. As the Captain, I had the largest room, though it still wasn't huge. It was divided into a more public meeting and dining room for the officers and my private quarters off to the starboard side of the ship. She sat at my invitation and I sank into a chair across from her.

"Captain, the Tribunal Penitents...."

"I know." I filled her in on our conversation in case she hadn't overheard. Her senses were almost as keen as my own.

"I don't like it."

I imagined her tail twitching in irritation, and tried to keep the smile that image prompted off my face. "I don't either, but there's not much we can do about it now. It'll likely come to a fight."

She grinned in anticipation. I was grateful her smile wasn't directed at me. Weres could take a vampire if they got lucky, and Kena was an excellent fighter.

"We're almost fully loaded. The aether is onboard. We have a few more supplies to take on before we can leave. We're on schedule."

"Excellent. Get some sleep, Kena. I'll handle the rest tonight."

"You really think I'll rest with those Penitents out there?" She stood and paced, unable to contain her restless energy. "They all need to die."

"Kena, relax." I stood and put a hand on her shoulder, trying to get her to calm down. Her shoulder felt hot under my cool hand. Weres had very high metabolisms and tended to be warmer than humans. "You should get some sleep. You have day watch while I rest and I need you alert." I couldn't read the expression on her face while she looked at me.

"Yes, Captain."

"Dismissed."

She nodded and I enjoyed watching her stalk out of my cabin.

"Kena?"

She stopped at my door.

"Do you need help sleeping?" I hadn't offered to use my mind control to help her sleep in a long time. Right after I'd rescued her, she'd had nightmares so bad that she'd almost jumped off the ship while we were at altitude. After that I helped her sleep for several months so she didn't hurt us or herself.

"No, thank you, Adair."

She was gone before I could reply. The softness in her voice and the way she'd said my name made my blood race and I took a few calming breaths before I went back out on the deck. I didn't know what that was all about, but I was still a little keyed up after feeding on fresh blood.

The ship was quiet for the moment and I made my way up to the pilot deck and leaned against the railing. I stood motionless and listened to the night. The quiet sounds my ship made while she rested at dock were normal and comforting. It was the deepest part of the night and most of the activity on the docks had quieted. The Penitents were gone as far as I could tell, and for a very short time, all was right with my little corner of the world.

A sharp clank from below decks and muffled swearing shattered the peace. I jumped lightly down to the deck and ran to the hatch that led to the engines. Basil swore again and steam hissed. The night watchman glanced at me but I shook my head and motioned for him to stay at his post. I slid down the ladder into the large compartment housing our twin steam engines. The aether gas gave us buoyancy, but steam made us go forward and provided speed for steerage and the heat to warm the aether gas. Steam leaked from a valve I knew wasn't supposed to be open. Basil struggled to shut it.

I snuck up behind the technomancer and placed my hands over his.

He squeaked in terror and twisted around. "Captain!" His voice rose a few octaves higher than normal.

I turned the valve and gave his hands the barest hint of a caress as I stepped back.

Basil had never gotten over being terrified of me even though he'd been with me as long as Makena. I'd given him every opportunity to leave, but it wasn't every day a technomancer got to serve on a dragon ship and Basil, a very proper young man from the Tribunal, chose to remain even though his captain tormented him. I was never mean, but he couldn't handle even the hint of a suggestion I might be interested in him as anything other than crew. Truly, I wasn't, though he was almost as cute in his boyish innocence as Kena was fiercely beautiful.

Robi called me greedy, I called myself opportunistic, but I'd never get involved with or feed on one of my crew regardless. Robi had assured Basil of this many times.

"Are you okay, Basil? You're bleeding."

He shoved his goggles back up on his face and touched the cut on his forehead. He blanched and pushed his sweat-damp wavy hair out of his face, smearing blood in the process. His eyes flicked back and forth wildly as if looking for escape. I stood between him and the exit, and I didn't want him to pass out so I took a few steps back. Basil relaxed a little.

"No, Captain. It's just a scratch. Um, I was doing some last minute repairs. Sir. Sorry, sir."

"Relax, Basil. Need help?"

"Um, no sir. Thanks." He touched his goggles as if to reassure himself they were still there, and then held up a wrench. "Just, last minute adjustments. Maintenance, stuff like that." His pale skin flushed red with heat and embarrassment and he shoved his sandy hair out of his face again. "Sorry, sir." Basil had grown in the last two years, his lanky limbs filling out with muscle from the sword practice we'd forced on him, and other work he'd done on the ship, but he still had some of the awkwardness of youth.

"Carry on then, Basil." I turned and left, smiling when I heard his sigh of relief. Poor kid. I made my way back up to the pilot deck and resumed my watch.

The rest of the night passed without incident. The eastern sky began to lighten by the time the last of our supplies arrived. Robi rose as the sun did, and the sturdy quartermaster efficiently managed the crates and boxes, getting the morning crew to help him stow everything. Robi was the quartermaster and cook, but he also acted as our healer. He could usually keep people patched up until we could find a real doctor

The sun rose fast and I watched the glowing orb flood the desert with life and light. Lethargy pulled at my eyelids and settled into my limbs. The sounds around me faded in their intensity and I fought the overwhelming urge to sleep. I blinked a few times while my eyes adjusted to the harsh light. Though I tried to plan our battles at night, they almost always happened during the day while I was at my weakest. Fortunately, my weakest was still more than adequate to fight a normal human.

Weres were another story. The Tribunal didn't employ any weres. They killed them, if they could catch them, so I didn't have to worry about facing one on a Tribunal ship. Other pirates were different, but they had to catch us first and Serpent Queen could outrun almost anything out there. There was more than one reason why I kept Basil around. The skills of a technomancer on a ship like this were invaluable.

Kena joined me a short time later, finishing whatever Robi made for their breakfasts.

"Did you sleep?"

"Yes, Captain."

"Good. As soon as Dana finishes eating, get us out of here. We already have clearance and I don't want to be late."

She nodded, and went below decks, presumably to get Dana. Dana and Robi were both part of the rebellion against the harsh rules of the Tribunal. Dana had joined me out of a lust for adventure, and Robi was with me because I'd needed his services and he'd been available. They were both from the northern climates and the harsh sun of the desert had turned their light skin red, though

Dana was worse off than Robi. Robi had some Cathayan blood in his background somewhere and that kept him from burning too badly.

Dana shoved a last bite of food in her mouth as she climbed up to the pilot deck.

"You could have eaten first."

"Kena's in a hurry," Dana mumbled around her food. She blinked her bleary eyes a few times and tried to straighten her wrinkled clothes while she ate. Dana was a heavy sleeper and I wondered if Kena had pulled her out of her hammock. She wore a light linen shirt that wasn't completely buttoned, and her heavy flight pants and boots. Her warm fur lined flight jacket hung over one arm and her flight cap and goggles covered her head. We were all ready to get out of here.

Kena was also dressed for flight, though she tended to wear a leather vest with no shirt underneath in almost all weather. It took a lot to make her cold. The rest of the crew on watch scurried about as Kena shouted orders. I supposed I should go change, but I could walk around in the worst winter naked and I wouldn't get cold, so for me, wearing flight leathers was more to blend in.

Serpent Queen strained at her moorings and I could feel her eager anticipation as strongly as my own. She was not meant to be tied to the earth anymore than I was and we both yearned for the freedom of the skies.

Pint scrambled up the ladder to the pilot deck just as Kena gave the order to cast off. "Weather is clear, Captain!"

"Excellent, Weather Mage. Stand watch."

"Yes, Sir!" She saluted.

I saluted her back. Pint loved being in the air as much as I did.

The moorings fell away and my ship lifted as the aether gas pulled her upward. As soon as we were clear, Dana pushed the propulsion levers forward and deftly turned the wheel, executing a perfectly smooth turn toward Cathay. We'd travel our pretend course for a couple of days, and then swing around to our actual destination, the wilds of the Tribunal lands. There a Rom caravan would take our cargo the rest of the way to the rebel camp. The individual aether canisters were small enough that heavy wagons could transport them without too much trouble. I'd have to accompany them for various reasons, which I disliked, but if all went well I'd be back on my ship in a day or two at the most and we'd be steaming for Cathay airspace before the Tribunal was any wiser.

Of course, things rarely went according to plan.

CHAPTER TWO

"It's time to turn, Captain."

"Go ahead, Dana."

The clouds—under Pint's control—hung, heavy and wet around us, shielding us from casual observers. The crew was used to running in clouds and I made sure they had warm clothing to hold off complaints, but none of us really liked it. Dana was a true pilot and always knew where she was going, which allowed us to run in clouds whenever we wanted. If she'd been to a place once she could get there again and she barely used the elaborate compass on the ship. Several of us could fly Serpent Queen, but she was the only one with that amazing sense of direction.

"Kena, you have the watch. Come get me if you need anything."

"Yes, Sir."

Basil intercepted me on the way back to my cabin.

"Um, Captain, uh, sir. I think you should see this." Soot smeared a dark line across his face and grease coated one sleeve. It looked like he would be sporting a black eye in another few minutes and his goggles sat askew on top of his head.

"Are you okay, Basil?"

"Yes, sir. Just, please come with me." His voice was surprisingly steady.

I gestured for him to lead the way. The steady thrum of the steam engines sounded normal and Serpent Queen, though lighter than usual, glided through the air with her normal ease, so I didn't think something was wrong with the ship.

I followed him across the foggy deck and down into the engine rooms. One of our marines held his sword and stood menacingly in front of an alcove between the two steam engines. The girl wedged between the engines and looking at us with frightened eyes was obviously not dressed for air travel.

"Go get Kena."

"Yes, sir." Basil scampered off.

I waved the marine back and took his place, studying the stowaway. Ragged, shoulder length blonde hair framed blue eyes, huge with fear, and a pale, dirty face. She reeked of old blood, but I couldn't smell anything fresh, and her light dress was ripped in several places. She flinched when I grabbed her arm, and hauled her out from between the engines. She struggled and hit me once but she quieted when she was in the open.

"Who are you?" I kept my voice hard though I could feel her trembling and sense her fear. I was glad it was daytime when my powers were weaker or I would have had a harder time hiding my reactions to her fear. Once I was sure she wouldn't try anything I released her arm and stepped back.

She rubbed where I'd left a bruise. "Katlin," she finally said.

"What are you doing on my ship?"

Katlin glanced around, but the marine's eyes were unforgiving. Kena and Basil arrived, and perhaps thinking another woman would be more sympathetic, she shot Kena a desperate glance. I knew without looking that Kena's expression would be as hard as mine. Robi followed behind and I had a feeling the only thing that kept Dana and Pint on the pilot deck was their duties.

"Well?" I prompted.

"I...." She glanced around nervously. "I needed to get to Cathay and I heard that's where you were going."

I crossed my arms. "We charge for passage on this ship."

"Please, I have nothing."

That was obvious. She was either part of the trap the Tribunal had set, or was running from something. It was hard to outright lie to a vampire or a were, and I thought she told the truth about wanting to go to Cathay, but she was hiding something.

"We need to eat too. Passage isn't free."

She sighed and hitched her shoulder up slightly, and then somehow her torn dress fell in a puddle on the floor and she stood there, naked. I kept my face impassive, though the thought of semi-willing food was enticing. I sensed her fear spike, leading me to believe this wasn't something she'd ever done before. Idly, I wondered if she'd make the same offer if she knew I was a vampire.

I glanced at Kena. A smirk played across her lips and she rolled her eyes at me.

"Katlin, put your clothes back on."

She blushed, even more embarrassed by my refusal. She hurriedly did as she was told.

"Robi, throw her over the side."

Katlin's jaw dropped. Robi looked at me over her head, asking with his eyes if I was serious. As soon as Katlin glanced away I gave a tiny shake of my head. He shrugged and grabbed her arms.

"But, you can't!"

"My ship Katlin, yes I can."

She tried to hit Robi, but he was bigger and behind her. I let Robi drag her to the hatch, and then I took a step forward and grabbed her arm, flipping her wrist over and revealing the small tattoo that said she was a friend of the Rom. I'd noticed it earlier and wished I knew for certain that it was genuine. The Rom would know, but I could only guess that most people weren't dumb enough to fake one.

She shook badly, believing Robi was about to send her to her death. Some ships would have, but fortunately for her, I wasn't normally that cruel, and I didn't think she was with the Tribunal.

"Robi, seems we have a mutual friend. Take her to the galley and put her to work. She can earn her food."

"Yes sir."

"And Robi, find her some clothes that won't accidentally fall off."

He chuckled and tugged her after him.

"Does he not like women?" I heard her ask as they cleared the hatch.

"Naw, likes 'em just fine. He's just picky. When's the last time you ate?"

I tuned them out.

"Throw her over the side?" Kena sounded more amused than anything.

I shrugged. "I wanted to know if she was going to start issuing threats. She could have been from the Tribunal."

Basil's eyes were almost as wide as the girl's had been.

"Good job, Basil."

"Uh, yes, sir." He touched his goggles then shoved his hands into his pockets. I took mercy on him and left the engine room. Kena followed closely.

"What are we going to do with her?"

"I guess put her to work in the galley. See if the Rom want her. Maybe take her to Cathay if they don't, and if she doesn't cause problems. As long as she's willing to wash dishes, she can stay for a while. Not like we're overweight." Dana's every other word was a complaint about how the ship handled with the extra aether gas on board.

"Surprised you didn't take her up on her offer."

I glanced at Kena. "You should know me better than that by now. Besides, she doesn't know what I am."

Kena seemed pleased by something, but I wasn't sure what. Hoping that nothing else exciting would happen, I went to my cabin while Kena went back to the pilot deck to fill in Dana and Pint.

***

Pint slept curled up on the deck box she'd turned into a second bed. Though she could maintain easy weather, like cloud cover, while she slept, I'd told her to let them disperse. She didn't rest as well when she was holding cloud cover and I had a feeling we'd need her at full capacity.

Moonlight bathed the deck in a soft silver glow. The sound of our engines would give us away if anyone was close, but we ran slow to minimize that, and dark so no one would see our lights. The engines' quiet hum and the refreshing cool air soothed my tension away and I tried to relax. The bright moonlight drowned out many of the stars, but the night sky was still ablaze. The sails were full and properly trimmed. The wind whispered through them, barely making a sound, even to my sensitive hearing. The perfect kind of night.

Something caught my attention. I concentrated, listening to the night, and I thought I caught the distant sound of another ship. It was muffled, almost as if I heard it through a fog bank, but the sky was clear.

"Pint," I whispered and shook her shoulder.

"Hmm?" She blinked sleepily.

"Go wake Kena. We have company."

Her eyes widened and she nodded, jumping to her feet and scampering quietly down the ladder.

I couldn't see the other airship, but I could sense the hint of life out there now. I suspected they were using magic to stay hidden.

Dana and Kena, fully armed and armored, joined me shortly and I heard Basil moving around in the engine room. The engines changed pitch as he readied them for speed. Robi would wake the marines and airmen, and then join Basil in the engine room with a few other engineers. Pint scampered back up the ladder and saluted.

"Cloud cover, Weather Mage," I whispered.

"Yes, sir."

"Dana, take the helm."

"Sir." She took my place.

I hated turning over my ship, but Dana was the superior pilot, and I was a much better fighter.

Close to fifty marines, humans and were-cats, crouched on the deck, taking cover behind the gunwale. The rest were below, preparing the cannons. The airmen and engineers went to their stations as Robi quietly woke all hands.

The clouds built up ahead of us slowly, seemingly a natural occurrence, and Dana steered toward them. A cannon boomed and I winced at the sharp scream of a cannon ball whistling through the air.

"Down!"

The crew ducked. The ball flew harmlessly over the deck. I heard the muffled boom of another cannon.

"Full Steam!"

Dana threw a lever and the ship jumped forward.

"Run out the cannons!"

I still couldn't see the other ship, but it was close. I could sense all the life and its crew was much larger than mine.

More booms.

"Dana, turn to starboard. The ship's off that way." I whispered and pointed.

Dana nodded.

"Kena, run below and when I give the word, have everyone fire. They might not expect us to know where they're at."

Illusions as good as the one hiding the other ship from view were hard to maintain and took a lot of energy from the caster, even with the ritualistic magic the Tribunal used, so we wouldn't have the element of surprise for long.

I shut my eyes and focused on the life I sensed. "Fire," I said softly, knowing Kena's sensitive were hearing was adequate. Moments later the roar of the cannons deafened all of us and Serpent Queen lurched sideways, rocking as the cannons recoiled.

Wood cracked and the enemy wounded screamed over the ringing in my ears. I heard a muffled "fire" and then the illusion hiding the enemy ship dropped. Dana gasped at the appearance of another dragon ship. Our maneuvers put it almost on top of us, but that was to their disadvantage. Serpent Queen's cannons had ripped the side of their hull badly.

"Dive." I tried not to let the tension I felt at the appearance of another dragon ship show. We could outrun zeppelin class ships, but we had no chance against another dragon class, loaded as we were.

Dana threw levers and spun the wheel. My ship dove, exposing her precious sails to the other ship's cannons, but they were still disorganized and the clouds thickened around us as Pint called more cover. The concussion of more cannons cracked the air and one split our topmost sail.

"Three hells, dive!"

"Trying, sir. This damn aether gas…." Dana spun the wheel again, cranked levers and steered us deeper into the clouds, and out of their direct line of fire.

I glanced at Pint. Her eyes were shut, but she showed no other evidence of strain.

The shouting and sounds from the other ship grew distant and for the moment we were clear. Dana also had her eyes shut as she steered by her internal compass. The front end of my ship disappeared as the clouds thickened around us.

Katlin, our little stowaway, dashed up the ladder to the pilot's deck. She was still inappropriately dressed, but at least this time her clothes wouldn't fall off. She shivered in the cool dampness from the clouds and wrapped her arms around her midsection, tucking her hands into her armpits. Her eyes were wide with fear.

"Go below," I ordered quietly, hoping, if she did speak, she'd take the hint and whisper.

"I'm so sorry, they've found me." She did whisper, but there was a hysterical edge of fear to her voice.

"Oh?" I stepped closer to her so she could lower her voice more. The clouds would muffle sound, but there was no reason to take chances.

"I thought they'd follow the other ship. The one I let them see me get on. How'd they find me?" Tears ran down her eyes and she was shaking. "You should have thrown me over the side."

"Why is the Tribunal after you?"

She shrugged. "I don't know. They said I had to go to their school, to wear their filthy robes, or I'd die." Katlin glared at me, defiantly.

"So you're a mage?"

She shrugged. "I can do a few things, not much. I don't know how they found out, but I ran. They found me in the Kingdoms and I managed to escape again in Kwadwo. I'm so sorry."

"Why didn't you tell us?" I crossed my arms and tried to look angry, as if we wouldn't have been attacked without her.

She flinched. "I thought you'd throw me over the side, or turn me over to them." It sounded like she thought the second option would be worse. I agreed.

Finally, I just shook my head. "Go below where it is safer, Katlin."

"But!"

"You'll be as safe as you can be in the galley."

Pint gasped and suddenly the clouds rolled away, vanishing as if they'd never existed. We'd gained distance on the Tribunal ship, but not enough. The extra aether gas slowed us a little, not from weight, but from a lack of it—it interfered with our ability to maneuver.

"Pint?" I caught her as she fell.

"Sorry, Captain," she gasped.

"It's okay, rest. We'll fight them off."

She grinned at me, but it was obvious she was exhausted. I hadn't noticed her struggle.

Dana cursed and threw levers, trying for more speed.

"Katlin, take Pint below to the galley. If we get boarded and things go badly, she's your daughter. Say nothing else."

If possible, the stowaway's eyes went wider, and she stared at me like I was going to eat her. "How'd...."

I'd had to move vampire fast to catch Pint. "Take her and go." I thrust Pint into her arms and glared.

She nodded, fear plastered all over her face, and left the pilot's deck with my ward.

"Adair, they're going to catch us." Dana threw more levers. "The rifts take that damn aether gas." She cursed and tried to cajole more speed from my ship.

"We'll fight, we'll win, and that gas will make a big difference for many people."

"The rifts take them all," she muttered, but I knew she wasn't serious. The people we were trying to help were her people.

26

"What happened to our clouds?" Kena asked, joining us. She looked around for Pint.

"Not sure. I think they have a weather mage, too."

Kena frowned. "Not sure I've ever seen anyone beat Pint."

I shrugged. "We'll worry about it later."

"Yes, sir. They're gaining."

"Prepare to be boarded."

Kena grinned and her dark eyes lightened to burnished amber as her jaguar surfaced in anticipation of battle. The skin close to her hands lightened to display spots that faded into her dark skin further up her arms. I wished she'd wear armor, but I knew that would hinder her if she had to shift completely. It was an old argument. She had laces up the back of her shirt that would split in case she shifted.

"Be careful, Kena."

"You too, Adair." She grinned, a toothy fanged smile that set my heart racing, and not in fear.

I smiled back, but I kept myself in check. She jumped down to the main deck and prepared her marines.

"Dana, make it seem hard for them, but we won't avoid them forever, so let them catch us on your terms. Do your best to keep damage to a minimum."

She nodded and kept throwing levers. We slowed a touch, and I moved to the back and watched as the other dragon ship approached. It was on a course for boarding. Dana cranked up the steam a notch and we jumped forward, barely dodging a volley of cannon fire. After the brief acceleration Dana backed off, making it seem like we were having a hard time maintaining our speed. Finally, Dana let them catch us. By the time the other dragon ship was broadside, we were more than prepared for a fight. I sent a marine up to help protect her and crouched next to fierce Kena.

"Grappling hooks!" I yelled.

The men tossed the hooks and hauled our ships together. The marines on the other deck looked startled, apparently not expecting us to take the fight to them.

I jumped onto the gunwale and gestured with my cutlass. The marines stood and yelled, waving their cutlasses. Though the enemy didn't show it, I could sense their fear at our intensity.

"Board!" I leapt over the small gap between our ships and dove into the crowd of men and swords, my cutlass swinging. I grunted as it struck bone, pulled it free and buried it into someone else's back. Blood spattered, the hot scent threatening to send me into a frenzy. I growled and the next man to fall left the world with his eyes wide in fear. That just made me grin more as I plowed through the enemy's marines.

Half of my fighters followed me across. The rest waited with Kena to defend our deck. I swung, gutting the man in front of me. He cried out in pain and fell. Blood and gore made the decks slippery and the air smelled septic as men and women died. I pushed my way through the first line, wincing as someone got a lucky shot in and laid my arm open to the bone. Fortunately my armor deflected a blow to my back, and my wounds began to heal instantly. One of my marines took down my attacker and I broke free of the crowd. The Tribunal officers were ready with their pistols. I shoved the marine to the ground, in time to save him from the volley.

I staggered back, grunting in pain as several of the small metal balls slammed into me, finding gaps in my armor. I'd heal, so I ignored them and darted forward, gutting one of the officers before the surprise registered on their faces. Blood coated my skin, hiding its telltale paleness and it was dark enough that, even with their gaslights, they couldn't see my black eyes. I mostly dodged a secondary volley, and it'd take too long for them to reload their guns. I killed two more before they could draw their swords.

My men took advantage of the hole I'd made and fought right behind me. I heard voices raised in chant and headed in that direction, not wanting to experience whatever magical badness they were trying to cook up. The good thing about Tribunal Penitents was that they had to use rituals to make their magic. The problem was, the magic tended to be very powerful once they'd completed the ritual. I caught the attention of one of my marines and gestured to the cabin. He nodded and followed me while the others dealt with the officers.

I kicked open the door and the marine charged in with me. My boiled leather breastplate slowed the bullet's impact but it still knocked me back. Fortunately they'd aimed for me, and not my marine. The Penitents were the two men from the docks. My marine used their distraction to cut one of the Penitents down. I recovered sufficiently and charged the other Penitent. He fought, pulling a dagger from somewhere. I twisted to avoid his thrust, but lost the advantage with my cutlass and dropped it, grabbing the mage's wrist and twisting it behind him.

"Captain!"

I turned in time to take a crossbow bolt to the side, instead of my back, and possibly my heart. I grunted in pain, seeing nothing but red for a moment as my control slipped. My marine shot the man with the crossbow and I sank my teeth into the Penitent's neck. Hot blood gushed into my mouth. I moaned in pleasure, losing myself for a minute. The screams of dieing men, the sharp clap of gunfire, and an urgent 'Captain!' from my marine brought me back to myself.

I let the dead Penitent fall to the ground and wiped my chin, though I wasn't sure why I bothered. I was covered in blood anyway.

"Sorry, sir. Think you're needed on the deck."

I yanked the bolt out of my side, grunting in pain, but the fresh blood helped me recover quickly.

The marine didn't meet my eyes, but I knew he'd stand at my back, and not stab me. He'd been with me for almost a year now. He followed me out onto the main deck. Most of the enemy was dead or dying. A few marines efficiently dispatched those of the enemy too injured to easily recover. A gruesome job, but necessary. Robi would have his hands full with our wounded and he didn't need to deal with theirs too. Others helped our casualties back to Serpent Queen or guarded captives. I would have preferred not to have captives, because now I had to decide what to do with them.

"Sir, this way." Another grim-faced marine gestured to a hatch. I followed him down into the dark hold, eyes adjusting to the low light quickly. Gaslight flickered under a door and I wrinkled my nose at the smell of unwashed bodies. It was an old smell, and I guessed this ship had been used for slaves or captives. The Marine led me to the door and I glanced inside.

"Rift spawn," I swore softly.

"Yes, sir," my marine agreed.

A translucent opalescent egg about a meter tall sat nestled in an iron and glass cage. It pulsed slowly with an inner light reminiscent of a slow heartbeat. I recognized the iron and glass cage. It was designed to contain and negate magic. The egg was a dragon egg. I'd never seen one, only heard of them. They were magical artifacts from before the Time of the Rifts and the Cathayans used them to summon spirits. It wouldn't actually hatch a dragon, being an artifact, but it was beautiful and held me mesmerized for a moment.

"Captain, what should we do with them?"

Them? I tore my gaze away from the egg and focused on the ancient man huddled protectively next to it. His hair, long, and gray, was braided down his bent back and his mustaches were impressively long as well. His dark eyes stood out against his liver spotted skin. He looked barely strong enough to stand and his hands trembled, but it was obvious by his fierce expression that he'd try and defend the egg if necessary.

"We won't hurt you," I said in Cathayan.

He looked surprised that I spoke his language, but my words didn't reassure him.

"So said the Tribunal."

"Well, that's the Tribunal for you."

"As you say. What then will you do with us?"

I hoped he meant him and the egg, because I really didn't need any other passengers. "Do you wish to return to Cathay?"

He nodded slowly, almost regally and I wondered if he had royal blood.

"Then, after we finish our delivery, it would be my honor to return you there."

The old man frowned. "And what payment do you require?"

"None, though I wouldn't complain if you thought well of us once you were home."

"We shall see."

I nodded. That was fine. As long as he wasn't going to have a fit right now, I didn't care. I was surprised he hadn't reacted more strongly to me. I was obviously a vampire, though the bloodlust cooled as the battle died.

"Get the egg to our hold and help this gentleman onboard as well. He is a guest." I'd have to get his name later. I had to deal with the captives. "Get any useful cargo over to our ship as quickly as you can and prepare to make sail, and send someone to Kena. Have her prepare a prize crew."

"Aye, Captain." The marine grinned. A ship like this would bring a large bonus for the crew. I briefly considered giving it to the rebels, but they already had a ship, and a Dragon ship would make them too noticeable.

The marines scattered to do their jobs. I headed for the deck to deal with the Tribunal captives.

CHAPTER THREE

Several officers knelt with their hands on their heads while my marines guarded them. Most of the rest of the crew was already dead, for which I was grateful.

They looked up, fear in their eyes, when I approached. My fangs had retracted, and my skin had returned to its normal dusky color but they'd seen me fighting earlier. Being covered in blood would have been enough though. The man wearing captain's bars glared at me.

"And you were following us why?" I stopped in front of him.

He managed to give the impression of looking down his nose at me. "You're pirates, in Tribunal airspace. Why wouldn't we follow you?"

"You followed me out of Ebony Kingdom airspace." I crossed my arms and glared down at him, letting my fangs extend again.

He remained silent.

I smiled, showing my teeth. The captain blanched, but remained silent. Shrugging, I slashed with my cutlass. The men nearest him flinched as his blood splattered on their faces. The smell of fresh blood was almost too much for me, but I maintained control.

"So, you were following us…." I prompted the next officer in line.

He swallowed nervously and eyed my blood soaked sword. I wanted to know if they were after the aether gas or if they knew about Katlin.

The officer hesitated too long and I slit his throat too. There were only two men left and they were both close to crying. I almost felt bad but I needed to know if we were going to be chased for Katlin too.

"We…." The young man's voice quavered. He was barely old enough to be called a man and I briefly considered letting him live. "We were told the rebels contracted you to bring them aether gas. We… We had to stop you."

"That's all?"

His eyes widened and I could see him searching for something else to tell me.

The other spoke up. "We're to keep our eyes open for a girl who escaped, but she boarded another ship!" The kid's voice broke in terror. "That's all!"

I tightened my grip on my cutlass. I had the information we needed, and we weren't equipped to handle this kind of prisoner. Other pirates and smugglers we could deal with. They'd stay in the hold, knowing they'd be released at the nearest port if they behaved. It was the way of things in the pirate world. The Tribunal soldiers were different though. They always caused trouble and I didn't have a real brig. I considered leaving them with the prize crew on their own ship, but that had its own dangers and a skeleton crew didn't need to deal with that kind of trouble.

They must have seen something in my eyes, because they both fell silent, eyes dropping to the deck in defeat. I glanced at my marines and I saw a flash of sympathy in their eyes before they noticed me looking. Both hardened their gazes and I knew they'd stand behind me if I killed the kids.

I clenched my jaw and swore to myself. "Get them aboard and make sure they are secure." Maybe the Rom would take them off my hands.

Both of my marines had comically identical surprised expressions on their faces.

I glared at both of them. "Go on then."

"Yes, sir. On yer feet." They hauled the kids to their feet and dragged them back to my ship. One of them looked over his shoulder at me and it seemed he wasn't sure if being taken captive was a good thing or not. I supposed that was fair. He knew I was a vampire after all.

I surveyed the rest of the ship, to see if anyone needed my help, but my crew had the looting well in hand. There didn't seem to be any other prisoners so I picked my way through the bodies, trying not to slip on the gore soaked deck.

"Captives?" Kena greeted me when I joined her. She looked unharmed, though she too wore blood.

I shrugged. "They're kids."

"They're Tribunal Kids. You're getting soft."

"You're welcome to go kill them if you wish." I half hoped she'd do it.

Kena's expression turned inward, as if she were considering it. Finally she shook her head. "No, too late now. Maybe the Rom will take them."

I laughed.

"What are we going to do with the ship?" She eyed it speculatively.

"Send it to your family in the Kingdoms? I'm sure they will pay handsomely."

Kena nodded. "And they have honor."

Which meant they wouldn't try to kill my men and steal my ship before we came to retrieve our crew and collect our prize. "Casualties?"

"Injuries only. A few severe though. They'll need medical attention."

I sighed. Our debt to the Rom would be high this time around. They'd fix my crew and possibly take the captives, but they'd want a high price in return.

"You're injured."

"I'll heal." I needed to clean up before I even worried about my own injuries. Robi could dig out the bullets once I wasn't covered in blood. He had others to tend to first. "Kena, break out the water barrels so we can get cleaned up. We're close to our destination, so don't be stingy."

"Aye, Captain."

I put the other ship out of my mind, Kena's skeleton crew had it well in hand, and turned to the business of repairing the damage to my Serpent Queen.

***

"Adair, quit stopping bullets with your body."

I winced as Robi pulled yet another chunk of lead out of my chest. "Would you rather dig them out of me, or train new marines?"

He went after another bullet and twisted his tongs while they were still in my chest.

"Careful." I growled.

"Put your fangs away you big baby. You whine like a little girl. Kena is tougher than you are."

I growled again but didn't argue. Secretly, I agreed. Kena was tougher.

Katlin stared at me, her eyes wide. Her normally pale skin was pasty, and looked worse than mine did when I vamped out. Robi had conscripted her as a helper for his healer duties and she held up well until Robi had time for me. Now she was almost literally petrified.

"Captain, sir!" Pint ran into the galley—our makeshift sickbay. "The prisoners were no match for my womanly charm. They've spoken."

I laughed.

"Hold still, damn it." Robi smacked me on the shoulder.

"Sorry."

If anything, Katlin's eyes got wider. Pint was used to seeing me and Kena get patched up, so being flat on my back on the galley table while Robi dug chunks of metal out of my chest didn't faze her.

"Robi's right though. You should learn to dodge."

This time Robi laughed. "Do what the lady says."

"Pint, I'm immune to your womanly wiles."

She batted her eyes.

Or maybe not. My heart melted a little. "Rift spawn, who taught you that?"

Pint grinned. "No one," she said innocently. I suspected Dana.

I sighed, defeated. "I'll dodge next time. Now, Weather Mage, report."

"Yes, Sir! I was defeated only barely, and only because they suspected I was aboard. Well, not me specifically, but a weather mage. They had to use the dragon egg's power, and they had to threaten to destroy the egg to get Grandpa's help." She seemed pleased that it had taken such a powerful artifact to defeat her.

"Grandpa?"

"The old guy." She bounced a little. "So I'm still the best weather mage in the skies." She executed a solemn bow.

"Good job, Weather Mage. Dismissed."

"Yes, sir. Captain!" She dropped any pretense of formality—it was all a game to her anyway—and took my hand. "Are you hurt bad?"

"No."

"He's gonna be when I'm done," Robi muttered.

I winced as he extracted another bullet in a less than gentle manner.

"Hey, be careful with my Captain." Pint pushed her lower lip out in an adorable pout.

"Do what the lady says, Robi."

He chuckled. "Pint, go get Adair something to drink before he decides to eat the crew."

"Yes, sir." She saluted. "He wouldn't do that, Robi." She called over her shoulder as she scampered off. "He needs the crew to keep Serpent Queen in the air."

I grunted as he extracted another bullet.

"I'm almost done, Captain." His voice had gone neutral.

"What's wrong?"

"Just thinking that Pint may have the right of it. You need us, so you don't eat us."

I snorted. "Well, yeah, I need you, but I'm not prone to chowing down on random people anyway. Bad for the image you know."

"Of course."

I could tell that wasn't quite good enough for him, but he wasn't going to press the issue. "Robi, I happen to like my crew. If you would care to notice the large pile of lead you've extracted from my body? I didn't have to take bullets for my marines. I could have let them die. I am fast enough to dodge, and this really does hurt. Some of it is responsibility. You're all my crew, so I should protect you as best I can. A lot of it is loyalty though. You've given me yours, therefore you have mine."

He stared at me for a moment, expression unreadable, before he nodded. "You're right. Sorry, Adair. Just, sometimes the kids speak truer than adults."

"She's got a point. If I didn't need you, I'd never put up with your abuse."

Robi laughed. "Yeah, well, one more I think?"

"Yes. You got the rest." I could feel the bullets like small pinpricks of fire, though I'd never told Robi that. I didn't think he'd be willing to leave me until last, if he knew how much they hurt.

"You all know what he is, but you still serve him?" Katlin sounded horrified.

Robi glanced over at Katlin, eyebrow raised. "Shoulda thought that was obvious by now. Whole crew knows. Can't deal, you know where the exit is."

She swallowed nervously.

I was gratified that, despite his momentary hesitation, Robi was solidly behind me.

"This isn't the Tribunal, Katlin. We've all sorts here."

She flinched when I spoke to her.

"Besides, he usually looks awfully good without his shirt on," Kena said, following Pint back into the galley.

Katlin's jaw dropped and I could feel her eyes on me, as if she'd just noticed. I studiously didn't look back at her, instead staring at the decking above my head. "Thanks. I think."

Kena patted me on the shoulder. The heat from her soft skin seared my shoulder and I shut my eyes and gritted my teeth, trying to ignore what her touch did to me, when I was so close to the edge of my control. She left her hand on my shoulder a moment longer than necessary, and then Robi went back to work. This one was pretty deep and I had a harder time hiding the pain Robi caused as he dug around for it, though it did distract me from inappropriate thoughts about my first mate. Kena slid her hand into mine and I squeezed it gratefully.

"Ah, got it."

I gasped as he worked it loose. His tongs grated painfully against my ribs.

"See, Kena is much tougher than you are. You're crushing her hand, and she hasn't made a sound."

I quickly released her hand. She shook it and arched an eyebrow at me.

"Sorry."

She snorted. "I came down here to tell you that repairs were proceeding well, all of the crew is recovering nicely and so far your captives are behaving themselves. Dana says we're a day out from our rendezvous with the Rom."

"Good. Thank you, Kena." The Rom would escort a few of us and our cargo to the meeting place with the rebels. Fortunately, they also had a relatively secure berth for us to dock the ship. Unfortunately, you had to be able to see in the dark, or be a true pilot, to find it. Between me and Dana we'd be fine. The berth was deep in a cave in the mountains, and a nice natural illusion made the cleft in the rocks seem much too small for an airship, especially one the size of Serpent Queen.

"Okay, enough of me without my shirt on." I sat up and pulled my shirt over my head, ignoring the lingering discomfort from my wounds. Pint handed me a glass bottle full of blood I'd purchased in Kwadwo.

"Thank you, Pint."

She saluted. I affectionately messed up her hair.

"Thanks, Robi." I gave him a friendly slap on the shoulder then left the galley, Kena and Pint right behind me.

"Gonna be okay?" I heard Robi ask Katlin.

"Do I have a choice?" Her voice quavered.

"'Course...."

Katlin's reaction to vampires, and me, was unfortunately common, and I really couldn't blame her. No one liked to be considered food, and at least on some level, people, humans especially, were food to me. Vampires were only actively hunted in the Tribunal, but we weren't truly safe anywhere.

Kena seemed to sense my dark thoughts and slapped me on the back. "Relax, Adair. We all like you."

"Thanks, Kena." I meant it to come out sarcastic sounding, but I didn't quite succeed.

"Why don't you take the ship so Dana can sleep."

"Who gives the orders around here?"

"Our illustrious captain of course. Now go relieve Dana."

I laughed. "Yes, sir, Captain, sir."

Kena smiled and went below decks. Pint yawned and followed me.

"You can sleep below, Pint."

"Someone has to watch out for you, Captain." She grinned impishly at me.

"Ladies first." I gestured for her to go ahead of me up to the pilot's deck. The sky lightened in the east and the sun would be up soon. I could barely make out individual details of the low mountain range we flew over. We weren't high enough up to need help breathing, but the air was brisk and all the humans had their cold weather gear on. Pint scampered over to her little box and stared out into the vast reaches of the sky.

"Dana, get some rest."

"Thank you, Captain."

I automatically checked the dials and gauges, made a minor adjustment and settled in for a few hours while Dana rested. Only the brightest stars twinkled in the clear sky, and lethargy settled into my limbs as the sun slowly rose.

***

Katlin came up onto the deck with breakfast for Pint several hours later, likely at Robi's request. She avoided my eyes, but didn't leave after she set the covered dish next to Pint's deck side bed.

"Where'd you get her?"

I frowned. "Pint? From a friend." I saw no need to tell Katlin any of Pint's story. Especially since I didn't know it all myself.

"Does she know you stole her?"

I arched an eyebrow. She sure was good at making assumptions. "Hey, Pint?"

"What?" She mumbled sleepily.

"Did you know that I stole you?"

Katlin's eyebrows rose.

"Oh, yeah, straight out of the cradle. You're a terrible person." She struggled out from under her fur-lined blankets. "Thanks for bringing me food, Katlin." She frowned at the stowaway. "You don't think Adair stole me, do you? Gosh, you're silly. I'm his ward. He's keeping me safe."

She never elaborated on her past, and I wasn't sure if she remembered much of it, or knew it was a secret best kept close. I never asked because I wasn't sure I wanted to know. It was enough that my lady dragon had entrusted the child to me.

"I've been with him for five years."

"Easy to brainwash a child."

I carefully locked the ships wheel then turned on Katlin. "I've tolerated your presence on my ship, and your distrust. I've fed and clothed you, and kept you safe. I will not tolerate any disrespect toward Pint. You don't know her story. She is with me for a reason, and it's none of your damn business."

Katlin blanched, opened her mouth as if to say something, and then turned and fled.

"I'm about ready to throw her over the side." I grumbled.

"She's scared," Pint said around a mouthful of her breakfast. "I was too when I first came to you."

The kid was surprisingly insightful sometimes.

CHAPTER FOUR

"A little cloud cover, Pint."

"Yes, sir!"

As long as no one thought too hard about it, cloud cover this late in the day in the mountains wouldn't be remarked on. Afternoon thundershowers were common enough, and Pint was very adept at building them slowly. As the storm rolled in, Dana brought the ship lower. I stood behind her and slightly to her left. I'd done this approach before, but the only time Dana had experienced the hidden docks was leaving.

She glanced at me. "You want to do this, Captain?"

"I trust you, Dana."

Dana seemed to notice that I didn't exactly answer her question, but the praise brought a smile to her lips.

Kena leaned against the rail just forward of the ship's wheel and looked out over our decks. The on duty crew stood on deck or hung in the rigging, ready for commands. Basil worked the engines and Robi stood ready to assist if needed. I didn't see Katlin but I sensed her in the galley. That was a good spot for her. My prisoners were secure below deck. Grandfather, as Pint called him, rarely left the egg. We were as ready as we could be for the approach.

Dana threw a few levers and Serpent Queen went into as steep of a dive as she could handle. I winced at a crash below decks—some piece of improperly secured cargo probably. I'd check on it later. One of the advantages of a dragon ship was her maneuverability. Dirigibles couldn't handle the maneuvers Serpent Queen could. Of course, the crew had to be prepared or they'd slide all over the decks. I smiled when I heard Katlin squawk. Everyone else hung on to handholds.

Dana brought Serpent Queen's nose up gently and we leveled out below the cloud cover. The storm overhead burst to life, showering us with rain as Pint let it have its way.

"Good job, Weather Mage."

She saluted.

Dana steered us toward the cleft in the mountains, glancing once at me to make sure she was right. I nodded and stood still so I wouldn't fidget, or try and take the wheel from her. She was more than competent. I noticed a few of the crew glance up at us as we headed for a space that was obviously much too small. I'd warned them about what to expect, of course.

Dana deftly steered the ship through the opening. I'd forgotten just how small it really was with solid rock a mere meter above the top of the mainmast and below the bottom of the hull. Serpent Queen's wings, fully retracted, barely cleared the sides of the cave entrance.

"Breathe, Dana," Kena said quietly.

She took a breath and some of her tension eased, though sweat beaded on her forehead. Light filtered in from the opening behind us, but darkness loomed ahead. Serpent Queen cleared the entrance and Dana sighed in relief.

"It's easy from here, right?"

I snorted. "Just be thankful you won't be able to see much."

"Thanks, Captain."

I grinned at her. "Kena, have them light the forward gas lamps. That will help."

"Yes, Captain."

"She's a bitch to handle with all this aether gas, Captain."

"You'll be fine."

Some of the tension left her shoulders.

Jagged stalactites reached down into the cavern, some so thick they formed full columns, meeting up with their counterpart stalagmites. Dana deftly guided Serpent Queen through the mineral maze as if she could see every one, even though our lights extended only a short way in front of the ship. I could see well enough to wince every time Dana came close to an obstacle, but her pilot ability was true and she guided us perfectly.

Dana cursed as the ultra light ship tried to misbehave in the still air but she wrestled it up to the dock where the Rom waited. Colorful lanterns welcomed us though I suspected there were guns trained on us too. This berth had served the Rom and the rebels for many years, and they weren't anxious to lose its secret.

The crew cast lines out to those waiting on the docks and we secured the ship.

"Throw out the boarding ladder." Even here Dana was having a hard time getting Serpent Queen to sit as low as she normally did.

I clapped Dana on the shoulder. "Good job."

She heaved a sigh of relief and nodded, wiping sweat away from her brow.

Pint grabbed my hand and followed me down to the main deck where a couple of Rom waited. Gas lamps hissed as we burned precious fuel so the humans could see, though even I needed some light. My hand twitched toward my sword when I didn't recognize the man and woman standing on my deck, but I forced myself to relax. As fast as I was, they had the upper hand here. I would probably escape with my life, but that would be it. Pint held my hand and swung my free arm, unconcerned. She'd always been a friend of the Rom. I'd had occasion to fight against them in the past before they'd named me friend.

"Adair!"

I relaxed at the familiar voice.

"Sorry I'm late. Damn horse threw a shoe," Stela said.

Pint released my hand and I hurried to the boarding ladder to help Stela. She was the one who had first named me friend, though I had no doubt her horse would have all four of its shoes if I checked. Something else had made her late, but she didn't want to explain.

Stela took both my hands when I offered them and she allowed me to pull her gently into the ship. Once she stood on her feet she hugged me and then led me to her companions. The garish colors Stela wore clashed with the bright orange hair that rippled down her back. Each of her layered skirts was a brighter color than the last, and her shirt and vest were brilliant even in the uncertain gaslight. Mischief danced in her green eyes and in the wicked smile that usually adorned her tan face.

"Costin'll be sorry he missed ya." She nudged me in the ribs.

"Where is he?" I was sorry I'd miss him, too.

"We sent him off to recon 'fore we knew you were coming. Ah, Bianca, Luca, this is Captain Adair and his lil'girl, Pint. Bianca runs the wagons, now that Valeria's stepped down. Luca's her second. I'm still in charge of…" she laughed, "foreign affairs."

That meant she was in charge of all the logistics around their smuggling operations, rebel activities, and everyone the tribe interacted with. Not all Rom tribes were involved in the rebellion against the Tribunal, but many of them at least had rebel sympathics.

"It's nice to see you, Stela. I didn't know Valeria had stepped down."

She smiled at me. "Some of us get old and retire."

"Right."

Bianca eyed me suspiciously. She had the same tan skin as Stela, but her eyes were blue like the twilight skies and her hair was as dark as midnight and cut chin length. She wore garishly patched pants and a shirt and vest that rivaled Stela's for color. With her dark hair, she didn't look old enough to run the wagons, but crow's feet at her eyes said that she looked younger than she was. Luca dressed a little more sedately in similar pants, shirt and vest. He wore his hair long and it matched his brown eyes.

Luca seemed more inclined to accept Stela's word that I was okay. He gave me an easy smile, which I returned.

"You've cargo for us." Bianca's stern tone left no room for doubt that things had better be exactly as Stela and I had planned, or else. She had a touch of the regional accent that colored Stela's words, but she would pass in Tribunal lands as one of the city folk if she had too. I wondered if she used to spy for her tribe. It was odd that I hadn't met her, or Luca before. I thought I'd known most of Stela's tribe.

"Yes. If you'd tell Kena where you want the cargo we can start unloading." I gestured to my first mate. Her eyes glowed faintly, reflecting the gaslight. It was eerie against her dark skin, making it look like her eyes floated in space.

Bianca nodded curtly. "Luca, inspect it and assist the crew."

I arched an eyebrow at Stela. It was insulting to suggest that someone working with the Rom would be less than truthful. Of course the cargo would be inspected, but discreetly. Or that's how they normally worked anyway. Her words were more at home in a normal port than here.

Stela shrugged.

Luca approached Kena carefully with his eyes downcast as if she were a wild animal. After a moment she smiled at him and he offered his hand before they went below. Interesting.

"We'll have your payment once delivery is made. Who's going with us?" Bianca clipped her words, as if she wasn't happy about any of this. I wondered if she didn't like the rebel group we were working with, or if she just didn't like being so actively involved. Then again, maybe she simply didn't like me. I hoped it wouldn't cause problems later.

"Dana and Robi, myself and Pint." Kena and Basil would have to hold down the fort while we were gone. It seemed unfair to keep Dana and Robi on board when they could have a chance to see their friends, and I had to go, though I hated leaving my ship. Pint tried to go everywhere I did, and there was no reason to deny her a chance to see kids her own age.

"Very well."

"There's one other matter I'd like to discuss with you."

"Oh?" Her voice went from hostile to curious for a moment.

"Stowaway. She has the same tattoo." I held out my wrist. "I hoped you could tell me if it was genuine."

She nodded and gestured for Stela to join us when I led the way to the galley.

Katlin peered out of the galley, watching from the shadows. Bianca studied her for a minute then held out her hand. Katlin hesitantly gave the wagon master her arm. Stela passed her hand over Katlin's tattoo and it flared for a minute. Bianca let go of Katlin's arm.

"Tis real." Stela said. "She's friend of an eastern tribe. Welcome, Friend." Stela hugged Katlin before the other woman could respond.

"Thank you," Katlin said once Stela released her.

"Why ya traveling with these pirates?"

Katlin glared at me for a moment. "I thought they were going to Cathay."

I shrugged, unperturbed.

"Tch, well, you're lucky Adair's a softy. Most would'a tossed you to the birds."

Katlin pursed her lips.

"All's in order, Bianca." Luca leaned down the stairway to speak to his partner.

"Good."

That settled everything for the moment. Normally, I would have offered refreshment but with Bianca's earlier slight, I decided not to. Instead, I led them back to the main deck.

"Pint, are you ready to go?"

"Yep." She grinned. Pint loved shore leave almost as much as she loved the freedom of the skies.

"Go get Robi and Dana. We'll leave soon."

She saluted and ran off.

Stela and Bianca watched Pint go. Stela put her hand to her face, as if to wipe away a tear. I frowned but something crashed below decks and Kena cursed loudly, and the moment was gone.

CHAPTER FIVE

Darkness filled the sky by the time we left the cavern, though silver moonlight filtered through the dense forest. We were on foot this time, though the aether gas and a few other supplies for the rebels crowded the wagons that clanked and steamed behind us. The aether gas made the heavy cargo wagons light, but the containers were small enough that they wouldn't make them float away. Pint swung my hand as we walked, singing softly in Cathayan. Now and again one of the Rom would glance at her and smile. The Rom, as a general rule, loved children, and usually spoiled visitors' children even if they didn't truly care for the adults.

"The sky is very far away," she whispered, interrupting her song as she stared longingly upward.

"We're closer to the sky here than we were in Kwadwo."

"There weren't so many trees between us and the stars there." She squeezed my hand, and then went back to her song.

She was right. It did feel as if we were further away, even though we were in the mountains. Craggy peaks and dense pine forests obscured most of the stars from view. I always looked forward to time on the ground, but it seemed like when I got there, all I could think about was getting back in the sky.

I picked Pint up after she started yawning and carried her until we met up with the main caravan. People called out and rushed forward to greet their loved ones, but their exuberance seemed more subdued than normal.

"Dana!"

"Quinc!" Dana rushed forward and her brother wrapped her in a hug.

"The Rom let me come with them so I could see you."

Dana laughed. "I'm coming to see the new ship."

He swung her around. "It's marvelous. Come on, I'll tell you about it." He pulled her away toward one of the fires.

"We'll rest here for a few hours, and then carry on with horses. Pint, you can sleep in one of the wagons for a while if you want," Stela said, smiling as she watched the happy reunion.

"Thanks, Stela." Pint grinned, yawned again and crawled into the back of one of the supply wagons.

"I meant one of the homes."

"She knows, but she doesn't want to be left behind." The Rom lived in covered steam wagons, large enough to house a couple and kids comfortably. Stela's was a bright blue with yellow trim. Multicolored banners hung from the sides and rippled in the slight breeze. Their cargo wagons were colorful, open versions of their homes.

"You'd never leave her anywhere."

I shrugged. "She knows that, but still, she worries."

"Come, join us at our fire, Adair."

Stela led the way to a small fire next to her brightly painted wagon. I sank down cross-legged and wondered what was wrong. As a general rule the Rom didn't share their problems with outsiders, even their friends, so I didn't ask questions, just let Stela lead the conversation along neutral topics.

"How long will it take us to meet up with the Rebels?"

"Only a half a day or so. They constructed their ship close, for that reason."

Close enough to make the aether gas easy to deliver. Not so close that they would risk giving away the dock. It made sense to me.

"The ship's finished except for the gas. Quite proud of themselves, they are. Their shipwright's famous."

"Rebel sympathies?"

"No. I gather he quite hates them. But the Tribune discovered his magical tendencies." Stela laughed. "So here he is."

"Ship sound?"

Stela shrugged. "Imagine so. You might have a look."

"Okay."

"Stela." One of the Rom from the cave joined us. "The horses are ready."

She held his gaze for a moment then nodded sharply before looking at me. "'Tis time then."

I stood and offered her a hand to her feet. She accepted with a smile. Outwardly, Stela was calm, but her palms were clammy with a cold sweat and I wondered what made her so nervous. I knew it wasn't me—we'd been friends for a long time. I hoped whatever it was, it wouldn't affect my mission.

***

"They're sad, Captain." Pint guided her pony closer to the horse I rode. Dana and Robi rode in one of the wagons as did many of the Rom. Their steam powered carts and wagons made horses largely unnecessary, but many of the Rom still preferred horseback to the steam wagons. I agreed. The horses were quieter and more comfortable. This group even had a few horses that would consent to carry me. Their horse master had to have a conversation with the one I rode, or so I was told, but the horse was steady beneath me and didn't seem the least bit bothered to have a vampire on his back.

"How so, Pint?"

She shrugged. "Don't know. It's strange, I asked to ride with Kace, but he's away right now." Pint pushed out her lower lip in an adorable pout.

I patted her on the shoulder. "You'll see your friend again sometime."

"I know. Hey, let's see what Robi and Dana and Quincy are doing."

I guided my horse after Pint as she went over to our crew's wagon. The sky lightened perceptibly in the few minutes it took us to make our way further up the caravan and I fought a yawn as the coming day sapped the energy from my limbs. I was amazed that Pint was still awake, and not cranky. She'd slept for a few hours but that was it.

The three of them had squeezed onto the bench and Dana leaned against Quincy's shoulder while they chatted happily. Robi held the wheel that controlled the steam wagon and looked half asleep. He shook his head, as if to wake himself when Pint rode up.

"Robi, you can't be tired. We're on an adventure." He grinned at the little girl. "You're hair needs a trim, Pint. Tell that rogue of a captain to take better care of you."

"I'm growing it out," she said with heavy dignity. "Dana and Kena say I'll be beautiful and I'll be able to get my own pirate ship, especially if I grow my hair out."

Robi arched an eyebrow at me.

I shrugged. "I've known more than one lady pirate." My dragon lady came directly to mind. "If she doesn't want to be mistaken for a boy any longer, I don't see why she can't grow her hair."

"Adair, even if she shaved it off, she'd not be mistaken for a boy for much longer. If you hadn't noticed, she's turning into a beautiful young woman."

Pint beamed at me. I stared back at her, shocked. In my mind she was still five years old and terrified out of her mind as I whisked her away from some unknown danger and into the skies. Robi was right though. The baby fat had all fled from her face and hours spent in the rigging, or learning all the aspects of flying a dragon ship had left her lean and strong with a wild look in her eyes that rivaled Kena's. My little Pint was growing up.

"Well, we can't keep calling you Pint if you're not pint-sized anymore."

She stuck out her tongue at me. "Pint is a fine name. I'll keep it thanks."

I traded an amused glance with Robi. "Pint it is then."

Pint nodded sharply, her hair falling into her face. Her aviator's cap kept it out of her eyes on the ship and I hadn't noticed it getting longer, just like I hadn't noticed her growing up. Suddenly, I knew how parents must feel, watching their children rapidly turn into adults. I wondered if it was worse, knowing you'd probably outlive them too.

Dana laughed at something Quincy said, breaking me out of my melancholy thoughts.

"We'll be there soon," Quincy said to all of us.

Dana nodded and I could see the excitement in her eyes. Like Robi, she'd left her life with the rebels to come fly the skies with me. Unlike Robi, she still had family here other than Quincy. Robi had lost all of his kin in a battle. He'd taken refuge from his memories in the vast emptiness of the sky. Dana followed her calling as a pilot though and I knew she missed her family.

Pint and I fell in with their wagon, and the rest of the trip through the dense pine forest went quickly. The trees muffled the sound of the engines, but the rebels had scouts and sent a rider to meet us when we drew close. He eyed the wagons, barely able to contain his excitement while he gestured back toward their camp. After a moment the rider took off with Luca. The caravan continued clanking and steaming along at its efficient pace.

Robi and Dana sat up straighter as we approached the clearing. I could hear the sounds of a camp waking up. Clinking pots, mumbled good mornings, a few excited shouts when people found out we were almost there. Pint leaned forward, peering through her mount's ears as if that would help her see the new ship faster.

We broke into the clearing. The rebel camp was bigger than I had expected. I didn't think there would be any families here, but almost fifty men and women rushed about their tasks or came to greet us. Pint looked around, wide-eyed. People shouted greetings and a few of the rebels waved at Robi and me, recognizing us from the last time we delivered supplies. The wagons trundled forward, but a few of the Rom who were already in camp came to take our horses.

Quincy jumped off the wagon and grabbed Dana's hand. "Come on, I'll show you my ship!"

She glanced at me for permission and I waved her on. She laughed and took off after her brother.

"Let's go see the new ship, Adair."

"Hop up with Robi. I'll join you in a minute, Pint."

"Okay."

Before she could move I swept her up and planted her on the seat next to my quartermaster. Pint scrambled up so that she was standing on the seat. She balanced with a steadiness born of years in the sky and grinned as she studied the airship that sat in the dry dock.

"She can't wait to be free!" Pint stretched her arms to the sky. "And we brought her that freedom. She'll love us forever."

"Be sure to tell her that we belong to Serpent Queen. That way she'll recognize us if she sees us above."

"I will," Pint said gravely.

She often spoke as if the ships were alive, and I had little room to argue with her. I did it too. I left Pint in Robi's care and went to find Stela.

She stood with Luca, the leader of the camp—a rebel I knew named Karl—and one other man I didn't recognize. He wore the clothes of an English gentlemen and the gear of a tinkerer. I suspected he was the shipwright. His spectacles were non-descript, but the belt and multitude of pouches he wore clashed with his gentlemen's clothing and the magnifying device, designed to be worn in the place of spectacles, hanging from his neck was more ornate than anything I'd ever seen Basil use. He was distinguished in years, but still vigorous and he had a firm handshake when Karl introduced us.

"Captain Adair, this is Professor Orrell Howland. He designed our ship for us."

"Charmed. I must say I'm amazed you managed to give the Tribunal the slip and deliver the aether gas. Supplies are no issue out here," he gestured to the forest and I assumed he meant wood for the hull, "but aether gas is something else."

"It wasn't terribly difficult." I didn't see any reason to mention the battle.

The Professor arched his eyebrow, as if he didn't quite believe me. Obviously he still struggled to come to terms with the company he now kept.

"Yes, well. As you actually have your own ship, would you care to inspect this one?" His tone made it clear that he felt I was likely the only person here who could properly appreciate his genius. Of course the rebels were fawning over him, but Orrell was right, most of them had never flown.

"I'd certainly like to see it," Dana said, joining us. Her brother—Quincy—was with her, arm around her waist. He was of the same build and general appearance as my pilot and I thought they might actually be twins. I'd never asked.

"Professor, would you do us the honor of a tour?" I asked.

He positively beamed.

***

The good professor's favorite phrase seemed to be, "as a man of the air, you will appreciate…" and variations there of as he gave us the tour. Apparently, my great appreciation of his ship offset my obvious anti-Tribunal stance, and being a pirate and smuggler. Dana, Robi and I all gave the ship as much scrutiny as we could and I was as certain as I could be that there were no obvious defects.

"She'll fly!" Pint pronounced at the end of the tour.

I was willing to take her word for it.

"And she can't wait to have her dirigible filled. Look." Pint pointed. "They're starting."

"Oh, I should go supervise. Please excuse me." Professor Howland hurried off, leaving us alone on the deck.

"Something wrong?" I asked when I saw Dana frowning.

Quincy, who'd barely left her side since she arrived, looked surprised. "What could be wrong?"

Dana shook her head, still frowning. "I don't know. Something…" she hesitated. "Something doesn't feel right."

"Is it the ship?" Quincy sounded alarmed.

"No, Quince. The ship is fine. More than fine, it's a masterpiece. Pint is right, it sings to me, ready to take to the air. Something else is wrong."

I looked around, but what I could see of the camp was calm. People hurried about, getting ready to take to the air, or break camp and return to their main base, but no one seemed alarmed. The Rom had gathered their wagons, and the empty ones headed back into the forest. There was nothing unusual about that either. Stela, Luca and a few others would wait to escort us back later that evening.

"Keep your eyes open," I said to my crew. "Something has felt odd since we landed, but we weren't followed or we'd have been attacked already."

"Unless they want the airship mostly functional," Robi said.

We watched as the dirigible rapidly inflated in the harness that kept it attached to the airship.

"Won't be too long before she'll float enough to be towed."

"Three hells," I swore. "And we're stuck on the ground."

Robi shrugged. "I could be wrong. Just a thought I had."

"Well, since we all think something is wrong, I'll go find Stela."

Pint followed me down the scaffolding. I was beginning to regret bringing her. She'd be much safer on Serpent Queen.

"Adair, how do we fight on the ground?"

I glanced down at my ward. "Same way as in the sky... just with more space, and less danger of plummeting to our deaths."

"Oh." She looked relieved.

"If something does happen, stay with me. I'll protect you."

"I know you will." Her liquid black eyes were filled with confidence in me.

Something akin to the earlier pain from the realization that she was growing up hit me. I forced a smile. "Come on, Weather Mage. Stela's this way."

The dirigible creaked and groaned, and then the rebels cheered as it rose above the hull, pulling against its harness. Pint and I paused and looked. Joy momentarily replaced my growing fear. Pint was correct, that ship was ready to fly.

"Come on, Pint." I jogged through the camp, Pint on my heels.

"'Tis something wrong, Adair?" Stela asked when we reached her small group on the outskirts.

"We're not sure."

"Well, your payment's in the wagon." She gestured to the remaining steam wagon. A box sat in the back and I had no doubt that it would contain the rest of our money. I trusted the rebels and didn't bother to check.

"Good. Now...."

Pint screamed. "Serpent Queen! She's in trouble!"

I stared at Pint, shocked. How would she know? I turned back the way we'd come and started for the horses.

"Let's go. Stela, we'll meet you and the rest of my crew back there, soon as you can."

Pint already sat on her pony.

"Adair."

The tone of her voice made me turn and face her.

"I'm so sorry."

I frowned, confused, and didn't even have time to dodge as she plunged a stake into my heart. Pint's scream chased me into darkness.

CHAPTER SIX

Hot, warm, magic laced blood woke me some time later. I groaned, clamping my hands around the slender wrist at my mouth.

"Adair!" Pint sounded panicked.

I snapped my eyes open stared at her over her wrist that she had pressed to my lips.

"Pint!" I released her and sat up.

She clutched her bloody wrist to her chest. "I'm sorry, Captain. You wouldn't wake."

She thought I was mad at her? "I'm only mad at myself, Pint. I'm grateful to you." I looked around as screams broke through the fog in my brain. "What's going on?"

"Stela staked you, the rifts take her. That bitch!"

My eyes went wide at her language.

"Then an airship came. Everyone is fighting now. The other Rom wanted to kill you, but Stela said they couldn't. Their betrayal was already too much, especially to one who was a Friend. I ran away on my horse until they went away from you. Get up, we have to help them. They'll steal Freedom."

It took me a moment to understand she was talking about the dirigible ship. The air sac wasn't quite full but it strained against its harness and it had more than enough buoyancy to be towed.

"Give me your wrist first."

She did so without hesitation. The sight of her blood was hard to resist, but I managed. She hadn't cut herself deeply and the bleeding had slowed. I hesitated, feeling bad about taking her blood, but the damage was already done. I licked the wound to help it heal more quickly. Then I ripped the tail off of my shirt and wrapped her wrist tightly.

"Is that okay?"

She nodded.

"Pint, I need you to hide somewhere safe."

She nodded again and scrambled into the forest. I took off in the other direction, running for the airship and the main part of the battle as fast as a vampire during the day could go.

The main part of the battle had already moved to the ships. A couple stragglers saw me when I slowed to dispatch them. They grinned, seeing me bloody and ragged looking and thinking I would be an easy target. I lunged, feeling steel grate on bone as I killed the first. The other's eyes went wide and he tried to run so I stabbed him in the back and sprinted toward the airships.

Bodies littered the ground, Tribunal and Rebel. I hadn't seen a dirt-side battle like this since the Rift Wars many years ago. It brought back unpleasant memories, but I didn't have time to dwell on them as I plunged into the fight. Even hindered by the sunlight, I was more than a match for most of the humans and I plowed through their ranks, my sword slicing through them like they were merely slabs of meat. The stink of blood and split bowels choked the air. Screams of dying men and women destroyed what would have otherwise been an idyllic afternoon.

I jumped halfway up the scaffolding of the dry dock, caught a beam and scrambled up the rest, throwing myself over the gunwale and into the fight on the deck.

Men tried to secure towing lines to the bow, while another dirigible airship hovered nearby. Its cannons pointed straight at us, but fortunately they seemed to want the ship intact and so far weren't firing.

I heard Dana shout in fury and saw her, Quincy and Robi fighting a short way from the bow. They were okay for now, so I cut a bloody path through the combatants, ignoring, barely, the blood that spattered up my arms and across my chest and face as I killed Tribunal soldiers.

Pint's blood was potent, the dragon blood that ran through her veins and fueled her magic gave me more strength than I normally would have received from the small amount of blood I'd taken from her. That wore off as I tried to heal the wound in my chest and fight. I'd need more blood soon, or risk losing control of myself. Fortunately there were many handy Tribunal soldiers to feed from. I just needed the opportunity.

I hacked and slashed with my cutlass until no one but the men with the towing line were in front of me. Perfect opportunity. I dispatched one quickly and punched the other in the face to give me time to hack through the lines. He dropped like a rock. Shots rang out from the deck of the other ship and zinged past me as the thick tow lines slowly parted under the edge of my sword.

I stumbled backward as a bullet slammed into my shoulder. My vision went red for a moment as my control slipped, but I had to get those towlines off. One more solid hit did it and they fell away. I heard someone curse on the other ship and I dove to the deck as a cannon boomed. Apparently they were done trying to capture Freedom. There was no way we could defeat the other ship, tied to the ground as we were. They weren't dumb enough to come into range of Freedom's cannons. Except this ship didn't even have cannons yet.

My vision hazed out again. I scrambled across the deck to the unconscious soldier I'd punched earlier and sank my teeth into his neck. Feeding during a battle was a good way to get killed. Fortunately, I'd had a lot of practice, and I had friends on the ship, so I took my fill then got up into a low crouch. No one noticed me. The cannons on the other ship had all their attention.

"Surrender," someone on the other ship called over a bullhorn.

The rebel soldiers traded defeated looks. Perhaps I should have left the towlines alone for a bit longer.

One of the remaining Tribunal soldiers shoved Dana to her knees. Robi followed, and slowly the others dropped their weapons. What else could they do?

I sighed as I heard the familiar snap of a dragon ship's wings. Of course they had backup. Cannons roared and I risked a look above the gunwale. That wasn't their ship. That was my ship! And she tore into the Tribunal dirigible with a fury reminiscent of a real dragon made flesh. It took a moment for the people on the ship to catch on, but when they did, they turned on the remaining

Tribunal soldiers, killing them swiftly. I ran toward the worst of the fighting.

Dana and Quincy stood back to back. Robi was to their right. I stepped over the pile of Tribunal bodies that surrounded them and stood to their left. A handful of soldiers attacked.

Dana lunged too far and slipped on the gore-covered deck. She cried out as she fell. The soldier she fought lunged. I thrust, ignoring the man I fought for a moment and tried to catch the other soldier's blade before it impaled Dana. Quincy turned at the same time.

The soldier behind me took advantage of my distraction and thrust his sword into my back. I stumbled forward, crying out involuntarily. I staggered, but kept my feet, spinning and splitting the surprised soldier from his shoulder to his chest with my cutlass. He fell and I turned again. I'd deal with the wound, and the pain, later.

Quincy lay on the deck, eyes wide, sword protruding from his gut. The other soldier was dead, Dana's cutlass stuck in his skull. He must have taken the blow meant for Dana.

"Quincy, no!" Dana held her brother. "Not for me."

He clutched at the wound, holding the sword. "Love you, Dana." He choked, blood spilling from his mouth as he tried to say something else, and then coughed his last breath.

"No!" Dana screamed.

Robi grabbed Dana and held her tight, despite her struggle. She punched him a few times, and then collapsed sobbing.

I clenched my jaw and looked around. The Tribunal soldiers were dead. Their airship burned, and crashed to a smoking heap on the ground. I winced as gunpowder exploded, sending shrapnel flying. More people screamed but the air battle was effectively over.

My beautiful Serpent Queen rested on the treetops. Directly on top of them. One of the taller trees threatened to tear her wing, others scraped her hull or bent under her weight. Who was flying her anyway? And how'd they get out of the cave?

Serpent Queen lurched, and then drunkenly maneuvered toward the clearing. I winced as the trees scraped her freshly painted hull. She settled in a clear spot, hovering meters above the ground. Someone threw out the boarding ladder and my marines swarmed to the ground.

"Robi?"

"I'll take care of her, Adair. Go'n find out what happened."

I needed to find Pint, and Stela.

Both turned out to be easier than I had anticipated. Stela wasn't far from where she'd staked me, a Tribunal sword stuck in her gut. She was still alive, but barely. Luca lay nearby, dead. I knelt next to Stela, the woman I'd called friend for years, anger burning through me. So many people dead. Why?

Pint appeared next to me. I glanced at her to make sure she was in one piece then focused on Stela.

"Why, Stela?" I asked once her eyes focused on me.

She blinked a few times, as if trying to recognize me. "Adair. So sorry. The children. Bastards took the children." She gasped, the effort of talking sapped the last of her strength and her breath rattled out of her for the last time.

"The Tribunal has their kids? They have Kace?"
Tears streamed down Pint's face.

I took a deep breath and stepped away from my fallen friend. I'd be able to forgive her, someday. I'd do anything to keep Pint safe, so I understood. She could have come to me for help though. We would have done something.

"Will we help them, Adair?"

"Maybe, Pint. But not today." There wasn't anything we could do now anyway. "Let's get back to Serpent Queen."

"She's hurt, Adair." Pint choked back tears.

"I know sweetie." I hugged my ward and pulled her to her feet. She held up her hands, and though I was covered with blood, I picked her up and carried her back toward our ship.

***

I could see the evidence of Serpent Queen's struggle to escape the hidden dock written in her damage. The bent wing struts, the torn sails, the broken foremast, all told a vivid tale, but she was still in our hands and the Tribunal had paid a dear price for their deception.

Kena met me at the base of the boarding ladder.

"The Rom betrayed us, sir." Her voice was short and anger and the stress of battle had turned her black eyes amber. Dark spots showed on her bare skin as her Jaguar tried to surface.

"Makena, the Tribunal has their children."

She actually growled. "No excuse."

I nodded, agreeing with her.

"We would have helped them."

I nodded again.

69

"The rifts take it all!" She knelt and slammed her fist into the ground.

I waited for her temper to spend itself and hoped she didn't shift. There was a lot we needed to deal with, and I wanted her help. She punched the ground a few more times then managed to get a hold of herself. She stood after a few minutes, forcing calm, regular breaths. Her spots faded, though her eyes remained bright amber.

"Sorry, sir."

"I know."

"They hurt my ship." Pint sounded angry and as hurt as the Serpent Queen.

I didn't even want to inspect the damage. "How'd you get out?" I would have left Dana with the ship if I'd expected any chance of treachery.

Kena winced. "Um. Basil, mostly… while I fought with the marines. Sorry, think we're responsible for about half the damage."

I surprised her by laughing. "Kena, if you hadn't come when you did, we'd be fighting a very different battle. We can handle a few repairs."

"We gonna get paid for this?"

Her mercenary attitude surprised me for a moment, but it was a practical concern.

"We've been paid, if our money hasn't wandered off."

"It wandered off," Pint said sadly. "Wagon's gone."

I put her down and she went and hugged Kena. "I couldn't stop them. I'm sorry. I tried, but there were two big men. I'm not so good at weather when I'm on the ground."

"Oh, sweetie, it's okay." Kena hugged her back.

I tried not to think about my ward trying to fight two men over money. "We got half. It'll be enough. We're headed to Cathay next. We can lick our wounds there and find more work. And we still have much of our other cargo."

"Yes, Captain."

"Let's get this cleaned up. Oh, Kena... Dana's brother was killed. Take it easy on her."

Kena's face went ashen and she nodded. "Three hells."

***

We didn't want to linger long, in case backup was on its way. The supply of aether gas was largely intact and the rebel ship was still sound, though it had a few unfortunate holes. Professor Howland was having fits over the damage, but despite the dramatics, he very adeptly guided the repairs. All the able-bodied men and women gathered the dead. Someone made a list, to notify families and anyone with even a hint of medical training tended the wounded. Dana busied herself helping Katlin and Robi as they patched up everyone they could. I lent a hand wherever I could and studiously ignored the hole in my back, the slightly healed hole in my chest and the bullet tearing up the muscles in my shoulder.

By the time we had everything sorted, I felt like I was going to collapse and though I paused to drink some of my store of blood, I didn't have time to concentrate on healing my wounds and they wore at me.

The rebels piled all of their bodies into one pyre and left the Tribunal soldiers laying for the crows and wolves. Someone said words, and a small group stayed behind to light the bodies, and then flee into the night if the Tribunal showed. The wounded, their supplies and most everyone else went onto their ship.

Dana stared as the last of the wounded were loaded.

"They have their own ship now, Dana. They need a pilot. If you want to go with them, I'll understand." I wanted to do more to comfort her, but I didn't know what I could do except give her the freedom to chose.

"Quince was going to be their pilot," She said, her voice tight with grief, but she'd cried herself out hours ago.

"I'm sorry, Dana."

She turned and glared at me.

I took a step back from the venom in her eyes.

"Promise me we'll continue to fight the Tribunal."

"Of course, Dana. You know how I feel about them."

"Promise!"

I took her hands in mine. "I promise, Dana. We'll fight the Tribunal as long as it takes."

She nodded sharply. "Then I'm staying with you. The rebels won't be ready to fight with their ship for a while yet. We're ready now."

I squeezed her hands and let them go. "I'm glad you're staying. You should see what Basil did to my ship when he flew it."

A hint of a smile touched her eyes. "Let's bury Quince. Then we can go."

I followed her to the small group of my officers. Everyone else was aboard and ready to fly. We'd kept his body separate at Dana's request, and Kena and I dug a hole earlier while we waited for Dana to finish helping Robi.

We stood silently while Dana knelt by the hole. Her brother lay wrapped in a cloth at the bottom of the hole. We hadn't had time to construct a coffin, but the Cathayan silk that shrouded him probably could have bought several coffins made out of ebony. I arched my eyebrows at Kena. She shrugged.

Dana threw a handful of dirt. Her breath caught. Kena put her hands on the Pilot's shoulders and that seemed to give her strength.

"He cared about everyone. He loved everyone. He even told me once that he loved the people of the Tribunal, too. He said..." she paused, gulping air and trying not to cry. "He said that most of them didn't know how evil the Tribunal was. He said it wasn't their fault. He was the best brother anyone could have."

Kena pulled Dana into a hug as sobs wracked her body.

I carefully shoveled dirt into the grave while the others watched. Every movement was agony, but it was nothing compared to what Dana felt.

Once I'd filled the grave everyone climbed the ladder until only Dana and I were left.

"Can I have a moment?"

"Yes, but I'm not leaving you down here alone either. It's not safe."

"Thanks, Captain." She sniffed and rubbed at her eyes.

I stepped a short distance away to give her time. It didn't take long before she climbed the ladder back to her home.

I surveyed the battleground. It always seemed more real when the fighting was on the ground. Blood couldn't simply be washed and scrubbed away. The smell lingered for days, or weeks, soaked into the ground. Battle scars took months or years or centuries to heal as the landscape was forever changed by our wars. This was minor compared to some battles I'd seen, but it brought back too many memories.

"Captain, coming?" Kena called from the deck.

"Yes, Kena." I groaned as I looked at the boarding ladder. This was going to hurt.

***

Smoke from the funeral pyre stained the air behind us as we steamed for Cathay. The rebels didn't have time to bury their dead, nor the space to take them on the ship, so they burned the bodies instead of leaving them for the Tribunal to find. The rebel ship headed in the opposite direction, deeper into rebel territory and hopefully to a better hiding spot.

The Rom's betrayal hurt, but I couldn't help wondering what the repercussions would be. Would the other tribes believe my story, or would someone else get there first and paint me as the traitor? I wouldn't have thought that way twenty-four hours ago, but now I wondered. We'd have to be very careful the next time we dealt with the Rom.

Pint was asleep in her little box on the deck and I leaned against the wheel, barely on my feet. Dana needed sleep more than I did, and I wasn't about to let Basil pilot again if I could help it. Much of the damage to my ship occurred during the escape from scraping against rock walls, though, to be fair, he was lucky he hadn't run the whole ship into a wall and destroyed it. He avoided me, afraid I was angry with him, and I didn't have the energy to find him and tell him it was okay.

"Captain, may I respectfully request that you go take care of yourself?"

I glanced at Kena. She'd been leaning against the gunwale, watching the night sky, since I'd taken over the wheel.

"What?"

"You're bleeding. Again. And don't think I don't know you're full of holes. And you never lean against the wheel like you're going to fall down if you let go."

"I'll be fine for a while. Robi needs rest."

"It's for our safety as much as your health, Captain." The expression on her face dared me to argue with her. "I'll take over here. You go get patched up. Besides, you stink."

I laughed, though it was strained. She'd had time to clean up. I hadn't.

"Yes, Captain," I joked. I mustered the strength to make my way down to the galley.

"Adair, you gotta learn to dodge," Robi said, obviously waiting for me.

"I dodged the cannon ball."

He laughed. "Come on, ya old pirate. Let's fix you up."

I smiled and hoped things would stay calm, at least for a little while.

The End

Doc, Vampire-Hunting Dog
By J.A. Campbell

My name is Doc. I am a vampire hunter – though I didn't start out that way.

***

"Hey Doc," Kevin, my human, said, slamming the front door behind him.

I winced at the noise. I never could get him to shut it gently. I grinned at him, then turned back to the sheepdog trials on the TV. I especially liked to watch them when Nelli was working. She was a master, driving the sheep effortlessly. I often had fantasies of working with her – flying over the fields as the sheep ran before us. It was a good dream.

I growled as one of the younger dogs made a mistake, wanting to show him how to do it properly.

"Easy there Doc, those sheep aren't going anywhere."

I snorted and settled back in the lazy chair. He was right, but oh how I wanted to chase them.

"This weekend," my human said smiling at me. "We'll go find some sheep this weekend."

I cocked my ears forward and tilted my head, asking for a promise.

"Promise."

We might not exactly find sheep but he'd take me out so I could run.

"I didn't get her this time," he continued, clattering around in the kitchen before coming out and scratching my ears. I licked his hand before going back to the trials. Joy of joys, Nelli was next.

A quarter of my attention was on my human but he was talking about hunting again. I never went along so I didn't feel the need to focus on him. He was talking about the signs he'd seen of his quarry. I watched Nelli as she effortlessly moved the herd, her black and white coat gleaming in the sunshine.

"You're drooling, Doc. Nelli on again?" He sat next to me and pushed a dish in front of me.

I perked my ears forward and grinned.

"Well then I won't ask to change the channel." I noticed him put the remote down out of the corner of my eye. He knew Nelli was my girl.

I barely heard the knock on the door, because Nelli was executing another flawless lift on the TV.

A sharp crash jerked my attention away from the TV. I grumbled in annoyance and turned. What I saw pulled all my attention away from Nelli and her spectacular run. A strange man had Kevin pinned against the wall. I wrinkled my nose. He smelled dead.

My hackles rose and I growled. How dare he invade my home! The man ignored me, snarling something at my human. Kevin struggled but couldn't reach anything to use as a weapon. The dead-thing was grinning, fangs bared.

I barked, trying to get the dead-thing's attention. He ignored me again so, despite my training, I charged at him. I had to protect Kevin at all costs.

I plowed into the man's legs, tangling myself in them and bringing him to the ground. I nipped at his heels as he moved impossibly fast, getting away from me. I snarled, baring my own teeth at the dead-thing. He laughed, meeting my eyes, then froze as I exerted my will on him. I stood between the dead-thing and Kevin, keeping him frozen while my human recovered. I pushed the dead-thing back with my gaze, getting him further from Kevin.

I heard him scramble to his feet and slide a drawer open. I held the dead-thing with my gaze, just like Nelli did with her sheep, while Kevin came around, moving slowly. I could almost feel the creature struggling to break my gaze, trying to get away but he couldn't. I forced myself to keep concentrating though it was getting harder, almost a physical effort to hold the dead-thing's black eyes.

Kevin edged around behind the dead-thing and lifted a sharp stake. I couldn't break my gaze to look and see what my human did, but suddenly the dead-thing fell to his knees and screamed.

Blood spattered out from his chest, coating my face. I jerked away, blinking goo from my eyes. The thing screamed again then crumpled to the ground, body falling to ash.

I stared, trying to comprehend what had just happened. I wasn't sure, but at least my human was safe. He was regarded me with a puzzled expression that probably mirrored my own. He pushed his glasses up his nose and smiled at me.

"I don't know what just happened, Doc, but you saved my life."

I grinned, happy that Kevin was happy.

He squatted down in front of me and, despite my gore covered state, buried his fingers in my white ruff and pulled me close, wrapping me in a tight hug. I tucked my chin under his and sighed.

"Didn't know that Border Collie eye of yours was good for anything but sheep," he said softly. "Maybe next time I'll bring you along."

I wagged my tail, happy to do anything as long as I was spending time with Kevin.

"Okay, let's get cleaned up. Then I'll find you some more herding trials to watch. Maybe we can even find some more of Nelli."

I grinned, perking my ears forward at her name. I licked some salty water from Kevin's face and he ruffled my ears one more time before leading me to the bathroom.

***

That is how I became a vampire hunter.

ABOUT THE AUTHOR

Julie writes fantasy novels and short stories about Vampires, Dogs hunting Vampires, Horses, and many other entertaining things.

Julie has been many things over the last few years, from college student, to bookstore clerk and an over the road trucker. She's worked as a 911 dispatcher and in computer tech support, but through it all she's been a writer and when she's not out riding horses, she can usually be found sitting in front of her computer. She lives in Colorado with her three cats, her vampire-hunting dog in training, Kira, and her Irish Sailor.

She is the author of the vampire and ghost hunting dog series, the Clanless series the Into The West series and many other short stories and novels. You can find out more at her website : www.writerjacampbell.com.

17646190R00046

Made in the USA
Charleston, SC
21 February 2013